# Welcome aboard!

# Other plays by the same author in English

A simple business dinner

An innocent little murder

Casket for two

Cheaters

Crisis and Punishment

Critical but stable

Friday the 13th

Him and Her

Lovestruck at Swindlemore Hall

Quarantine

Running on Empty

Strip Poker

The Worst Village in England

JEAN-PIERRE MARTINEZ

# Welcome aboard!

English translation by
*Anne-Christine Gasc*

La Comédiathèque
*comediatheque.net*

# Characters

**The young**
Natalie: Director
Roberto: Doctor
Christian: Blanche's son
Caroline: Nursing assistant

**The elderly**
Blanche: New resident
Harold: Resident
Harriet: Resident
Reggie: Resident



© La Comédiathèque
ISBN 978-2-37705-876-1

# Morning

*A living room, containing a few pieces of furniture, including four armchairs and a coffee table, giving the appearance of an outdated waiting room. Christian, a middle-aged man, is sat in one of the chairs, waiting. To control his anxiety, he randomly grabs one of the magazines from the coffee table and thumbs it. His mobile phone rings and he picks up.*

**Christian** – Hello? Yes, yes, I just got here, I'm waiting to see the director ... Listen, I really hope they take her in because I have no idea what we'll do with her ... Yes, I know I sound like I'm surrendering a pet to a shelter before going on holiday, but well ... I'm sure it's easier to find a dog kennel in Greater London ... At the very least it would be cheaper, because when you go private, let me tell you ... No, this is really the last option we have left... I have to play this right ... What other care homes? She got kicked out of every single one within a 50-mile radius! We can't board her away in Wales! Can you imagine the commute when we have to go see her once in a while ... *(Looking around him)* ... Well, I think it looks fine, but anyway, it's not like we really have a choice anymore. And it's not a done deal, you know ... The director said we were on their waiting list, but she was hoping that a place will be freed shortly ... Yes, I know it's a Catholic home ... Yes, I promise to watch what I say. I don't think they're extremists, but still ... Better make sure the odds are in our favour ... Listen, I've got to go, I think she's coming ... I'll call you back ...

*Natalie, the director, enters the room. She is between thirty and forty years old and is dressed like a posh Catholic headmistress.*

**Christian** – Ah, good morning, Madam!

**Natalie** – I'm sorry to keep you waiting.

**Christian** – Not at all, not at all ... Christian Martinez.

*Christian shakes Natalie's hand with a courtesy that looks a bit forced.*

**Natalie** – Natalie San Pellegrino.

**Christian** – Like the water?

**Natalie** – Yes, but before being a fancy brand of water it used to mean "holy pilgrim", you know.

**Christian** – Sparkling… Who knows, maybe the Almighty heard your pilgrim's prayers ... I hope you have good news for us, Madam the Director ...

**Natalie** – Yes, yes, actually we do ... I mean, when I say good news ... You know what they say, one man's loss is another man's gain ...

**Christian** – You have no idea how relieved I am to hear this ... Thank you so much for giving her another chance ...

**Natalie** – I have to say, she is a little ... lively, but well ... At her age, it could be a lot worse, couldn't it?

**Christian** – Back in the day, when my parents took care of their parents, it wasn't like that at all ... they used to be more ... docile ... It must be the new generation ...

**Natalie** – Probably the dying aftershocks of their hippie activist days.

**Christian** – Also ... don't hesitate to set firm boundaries from the start. You know ... if you feel it's necessary. To establish your authority. Or you won't he able to handle her later ...

**Natalie** – Don't worry, we've done this before ... We are professionals after all ... She'll be perfectly happy here with us ...

**Christian** – Oh, it's not her welfare I was concerned about ... And so, er ... you can take her in today, right…?

**Natalie** – As long as she has an overnight bag with all her things… You can bring the rest later ...

**Christian** – Oh, you better believe we packed her a full suitcase in case you could take her off our hands immediately ... I mean ... in case we could leave her in your capable hands immediately ...

**Natalie** – Right, well, you can bring her in now ... You left her with Caroline, right?

**Christian** – Yes, yes, I'll get her right away ...

*Christian leaves and returns a second later, a suitcase in one hand and holding Blanche, an old lady, by the other.*

**Natalie** – Blanche, let me be the first to welcome you to our assisted living facility, The Daisies.

**Blanche** – To remind us we'll soon be pushing up daisies?

**Natalie** *(sweetly strict)* – But you're going to have to be a good girl if you want to stay with us, Blanche. I had a look at your file and reading between the lines I get the impression you have a rather ... fiery personality.

**Christian** – You heard what the nice lady said, Mum? There's no setting fire to The Daisies like you did at the Daffodils. *(To Natalie)* That's the name of her old care home, the one she got kicked out of for disciplinary reasons . . . *(Natalie seems a little surprised and Christian tries to backpedal a bit.)* Her responsibility was never fully established during the arson investigation… but still… maybe keep her away from matches ...

**Natalie** – Thank you for the heads-up, either way ...

**Christian** – Apart from that she can be really lovely at times, you'll see. Very sociable. Even funny, sometimes.

**Natalie** – Humour is very important.

**Christian** – She'll surprise you, you'll see.

**Natalie** – In any case, you were very lucky ... If you had contacted us just a month ago there wouldn't have been a single room available ... But as it happens, I've just had three come available all at once ...

**Christian** – Bad luck always comes in threes as they say…

**Natalie** – Unfortunately ... But what can we do? They are now at peace with the Lord ...

**Christian** – Let's hope there's enough room for them up there ...

**Natalie** – Saint Peter also has waiting lists for those who don't quite meet the entrance criteria, you know … It's called the purgatory …

**Blanche** – I thought it was called The Daisies ...

**Christian** – Come now Mum, this is an assisted living facility ...

**Natalie** – So Blanche, your son tells me you were an actress, is that right? I mean, before ...

**Christian** – And what an actress... You'll find out soon enough, unfortunately ... However, she now has a tendency to forget her lines, even when she's not acting, isn't that right Blanche?

**Blanche** – So if I die, I can't be buried with the others?

**Christian** – Why would you say something like that ...?

**Blanche** – Don't you Catholics refuse to bury actors in your cemeteries?

**Natalie** – You know Blanche, the Catholic Church has considerably evolved on that point ... And on several others too ... We now accept that a bad actor can be a good Catholic ...

**Blanche** – Even the Jewish ones?

**Christian** – Mum, please, no one is getting buried any time soon ... And you're only Jewish through your Dad, so it doesn't count.

**Blanche** – That's not what the Gestapo thought during the war.

**Christian** – Please ignore her, she spent the war in a farm in the countryside with her maternal grandmother. The only nazis she ever saw were on TV, in *Dad's Army*. But she loves to ham it up. Actors, what can I say ...

**Blanche** *(to Natalie)* – You're not in the Gestapo, are you?

**Christian** – Mum, please! You can see this lady isn't from the Gestapo. And I'm certain that, should the situation arise, as a last resort, she wouldn't refuse to give you the last rites ...

**Natalie** – But you're the picture of health, Blanche!

**Christian** – She'll bury us all, you'll see.

*Embarrassed silence.*

**Christian** – So, er, well ... I'll be on my way, right Mum? Before the director changes her mind ... *(To Natalie)* Now that I know my mother is in good hands.

**Natalie** – Don't worry, everything will be fine.

**Christian** – Right, bye Mum, I'll come back to visit you soon, ok? And be good. *(Feeling very emotional despite it all, he kisses his mother)* Thank you again ... I'll see you soon ...

*Christian leaves discretely. Blanche watches him leave, expressionless. Then she turns towards Natalie.*

**Blanche** – Who's that? Why does he call me Mum?

*Natalie looks at her, a little embarrassed.*

**Natalie** – But Blanche, that's Christian, your son.

**Blanche** – I know, I was just pulling your leg ...

**Natalie** *(relieved)* – Right ... Follow me, I'll show you to your room ...

*Natalie takes the suitcase and they start to leave.*

**Blanche** – So you're really not from the Gestapo?

*Natalie looks at her, wondering whether she's joking or not. They leave.*

*Reggie, an old man poorly dressed, enters at a stately pace, or even with a walking frame. He sits in one of the armchairs and starts to read one of the magazines,* Blue Rinse Life. *Harriet, another OAP, enters. She is also in a pitiful state.*

**Reggie** – Good morning Harriet, and how are you today?

**Harriet** – Oh, my poor Reggie, you know what they say. Past eighty years old, if you wake up one day and you're not hurting somewhere it's because you're dead.

**Reggie** – That's very true, very true ... Speaking of which, did you hear about Delia?

**Harriet** – Delia? No, did something happen to her?

**Reggie** – Oh yes, something happened to her all right… In fact, it's the last thing that will ever happen to her. She died!

**Harriet** – She died?

**Reggie** – In her sleep ... They found her this morning, stiff like a log ...

**Harriet** – No way ... And I was just speaking to her yesterday evening. I even wished her a good night!

**Reggie** – Well, that didn't work out so well, did it? If I see you me this evening, please don't wish me anything.

**Harriet** – But you're still so very young, Reggie. How old are you now?

**Reggie** – I'm going on my ninety sixth birthday. Not fast, but I'm getting there ...

**Harriet** – Oh right, I thought you were younger than me.

**Reggie** – Yep ... It had to happen one day.

**Harriet** – What did?

**Reggie** – For Delia! She was a hundred-and-three after all.

**Harriet** – We just celebrated her birthday.

**Reggie** – You couldn't see the cake for all the candles.

**Harriet** – Is there even anything to look forward to when you're a hundred-and-three years old?

**Reggie** – Apart from becoming an entry in the Guinness *World Records* ...

**Harriet** – Still, it's a shock.

**Reggie** – C'est la vie ... No one lives forever ...

**Harriet** – Not yet, unfortunately ...

**Reggie** – Not yet?

**Harriet** – You haven't seen that article in *Blue Rinse Life*?

**Reggie** – Which one?

**Harriet** – The one about this species of jellyfish that never dies.

**Reggie** – Jellyfish?

**Harriet** – Turritopsis Nutricula.

**Reggie** – Toast and Nutella?

*Harriet takes the magazine from him, looks for the article and finds it.*

**Harriet** – Listen to this *(reading)*: According to biologists, it is currently the only living creature known for being immortal. After reaching adulthood, this jellyfish can revert its ageing cells back to their original state, thus achieving a form of eternal youth. Only recently discovered, these jellyfish can be found in the deepest oceans. However, since they are immortal, they multiply uncontrollably, creating barely contained panic among the scientific community. "The world needs to be prepared to face this silent invasion", said a visibly shaken marine biologist.

**Reggie** – A silent invasion? What's the name of this scientist facing the invaders ...? Doctor Who?

**Harriet** – But do you understand what that means? Maybe one day they'll be able to transplant a couple of genes from these critters in our bodies and we'll become immortal too!

**Reggie** – Or they'll throw us in overcrowded tanks in a fish farm and harvest eternally fresh sushi ... Apparently, jellyfish sushi is a delicacy in Japan.

**Harriet** – Maybe that's why they live so long ...

**Reggie** – Seriously, Harriet! Every year they remind us that the state pension is on the verge of bankruptcy because we live too long! To them, we're the invasion! We, the senior citizens! Do you think they're going to splice jellyfish cells in our DNA so we can live forever?

**Harriet** – We can always dream. What else do we have left, at our age?

**Reggie** – Dream to be turned into ectoplasm ... What does a jellyfish look like, anyway?

**Harriet** – Pardon?

**Reggie** *(louder)* – A jellyfish, what does it look like?

**Harriet** – Spineless, flabby ... It can barely see, can't hear at all and is very irritating ...

**Reggie** – In that case, I take it back ... There's still hope for you, Harriet ... I think they might have already spliced a good piece of it without telling you.

**Harriet** – What are you like ... Such a joker ...

*Reggie returns to his magazine, while Harriet sits in her armchair and sticks an earphone in her ear. Harold, another OAP arrives. He looks in better health than the other two, and is dressed more elegantly than Reggie.*

**Reggie** – Oh look, it's the captain.

**Harold** – Madam, Sir, top of the morning to you ...

*Reggie and Harriet become more animated now that the old playboy has arrived.*

**Harriet** – Good morning to you, Baron!

**Reggie** – Good morning, Captain! Did you sleep well?

**Harold** – Like a baby. And yourself?

**Reggie** – Oh you know, at my age ... Getting a good night's sleep isn't nearly as important as waking up in the morning ...

**Harold** – This new hairdo is ravishing, Harriet ...

**Harriet** – Pardon?

**Harold** *(louder)* – I said, this new hairdo is ravishing!

**Reggie** – You must be blind ...

**Harold** – And she must be deaf ...

*Harrier removes the earbud she had in her ear.*

**Reggie** – And now she's removing her hearing aid ... things are about to get loud ...

**Harriet** – It's not a hearing aid! It's the iPod my grandson gave me for my birthday.

**Harold** – Oh, right ...

**Reggie** – What's an iPod?

**Harold** – I haven't a clue ... Anyway, have you heard?

**Reggie** – Heard what?

**Harriet** – What?

**Reggie** – See, deaf as a post.

**Harriet** – I didn't hear anything.

**Harold** – Have you heard the news! We have a new resident!

**Reggie** – Oh, the one who's replacing Delia.

**Harold** – Delia left?

**Reggie** – Er yes, permanently.

**Harriet** – And swiftly.

**Reggie** – She didn't even have time to stop by reception to say she was leaving.

**Harriet** – That's not surprising, she was getting very absent-minded.

**Reggie** – Well now she's absent-bodied. She died.

**Harold** – She died?

**Harriet** – During the night, apparently ... And to think I saw her just yesterday evening ... I even wisher her ...

**Harold** – Oh bother, I forgot my glasses ...

*Harold leaves. Blanche enters without passing him.*

**Reggie** – Ah, there she is ...

**Harriet** – Who, Delia?

**Reggie** – The new resident!

**Harriet** – How do you know she's the new resident?

**Reggie** – Oh, for the love of God, because we've never seen her before!

**Harriet** – Maybe we've seen her before and we can't remember ... What's it called again, that disease where you forget everything ...

**Reggie** – Oh yes ... I can never remember.

**Harriet** – Something complicated, with a Z and an H ...

**Reggie** – I'm sure they do it on purpose, so us old folk can't remember what it's called ...

*Blanche enters. The other two display a slightly affected politeness.*

**Reggie** – Good morning, Madam. Welcome.

**Blanche** *(scowling)* – Have we met ...?

**Reggie** – I don't think so ...

**Harriet** – Please, won't you sit with us for a bit.

*As Harriet stands to pull an armchair for Blanche, Blanche sits in Harriet's chair. Harriet turns around and realises Blanche took her place.*

**Harriet** – I'm sorry ... I mean ... This is my chair ...

**Blanche** – I don't see your name on it ...

*Harriet looks distraught, but Blanche remains seated.*

**Reggie** – It's her favourite chair ...

**Blanche** – So what? Sitting in a different armchair in a retirement home is like sitting in a different deck chair on the Titanic, isn't it?

**Harriet** – Funny you should say that, because I was there, you know ...

**Blanche** – Where?

**Harriet** – On the Titanic!

**Reggie** – Please, don't get her started ... She can't remember what she had for breakfast this morning but she can tell you every detail of the sinking of the Titanic. Down to the menu served at the captain's table and the set list for the orchestra.

**Blanche** – The Titanic ... How old were you?

**Harriet** – Three months old. But you know how it is, when age starts affecting your memory, the oldest memories come to the surface.

**Reggie** – In a year or two she'll be able to tell us about her mother giving birth.

**Blanche** – And on her deathbed she'll be describing her conception ...

**Reggie** – Good God ...

**Harriet** – Have you heard about those immortal jellyfish?

**Blanche** – The Turrotopsis Nutricula ...

**Harriet** – We read about it in *Blue Rinse Life*. And did you see this? If you correctly answer three questions on jellyfish you can win a cruise. Well, there's a draw of course ...

**Reggie** – A cruise? On a ship?

**Blanche** – Yes, genius, on a ship! It's a cruise! Not in a bus ...

*Reggie looks at the magazine.*

**Reggie** – Swimming with jellyfish ... That's not a type of themed cruise you see very often ... Can you swim ?

**Harriet** – I'd go on another cruise. I rather enjoyed myself last time.

**Blanche** – You've been on a cruise?

**Harriet** – I just told you! On the Titanic!

*Harold returns, wearing his glasses.*

**Harold** – Oh, but I see we have someone new among us ... Let me introduce myself, I am Harold Featherstonehaugh, pronounced Fanshaw.

**Blanche** – Blanche ... pronounced Blanche.

**Harriet** – That's right ... And I am Harriet, pronounced Harriet ...

**Harold** – I'm just explaining how to pronounce my name.

**Reggie** *(grovelling)* – Harold is a little bit of a titled gentleman.

**Blanche** – He sounds more like an entitled tosser to me.

**Harold** – I was just explaining my last name is pronounced Fanshaw.

**Blanche** – Yeah, I get it. And I'm explaining you're already a pain in my backside, pronounced arse.

*The others all look a little shocked.*

**Reggie** – Come now, Blanche. Harold was a captain in the army.

**Harriet** – He was in charge of a whole boat.

**Harold** – I was a captain in the infantry.

**Blanche** – An army man ... No wonder you look less run down than the other two. You never worked a day in your life ...

**Harold** – I retired from active duty at forty-eight years old. That's one of the advantages of the army.

**Reggie** – He's been retired for almost half a century.

**Blanche** – And you wonder why the government's pension fund is close to bankruptcy. This place must bring you right back to when you lived in barracks, am I right?

*Caroline, a nursing assistant in her thirties enters. She is a super-bimbo wearing a white lab coat.*

**Harold** – Oh, Caroline! It's always so wonderful to see you. Even if the sight of you does dangerous things to my blood pressure ...

**Caroline** – Come now, Captain, I wouldn't want to break your heart ...

**Harold** – Alas, there comes a time in a man's life where this expression is to be taken literally ...

**Caroline** – I see you've already made some new friends, Blanche ... That's good ... Blanche will be taking the room of ... a resident who had to leave us, unfortunately.

**Blanche** – Lucky her ... Did she manage to escape?

**Caroline** – Yes, you could say that. Did you find everything you need in your room? If you're missing anything, just let me know.

**Blanche** – Well, since you ask ... I started digging a tunnel but I hit a concrete slab. Could you find me a jackhammer?

**Caroline** – Oh Blanche, something tells me having you with us is never going to be boring. Right everyone, it's time to get ready for lunch ...

**Blanche** – Lunch? But it's ten thirty? I just barely finished my coffee!

**Caroline** – Early to lunch, early to nap! That's our motto.

**Blanche** – What bullshit motto…

**Harriet** – Lunch is served at noon.

**Reggie** – At our age we need at least an hour to prepare ourselves just to the idea of having lunch ... and a solid two – or three – hour nap to digest before dinner.

**Harriet** – The day just flies by ...

**Harold** – Blanche, won't you have lunch at my table? That way we can get to know one another a little better ...

**Reggie** – Your table?

**Harriet** – The captain's table?

**Harold** – Well, yes ... Since Delia has left us, her place is available, isn't it?

**Harriet** – It's just that ... I was planning to sit there.

**Reggie** – That was the plan ... There's a waiting list ...

**Harold** – In that case, I'm sure you will gladly give up your place for Blanche, won't you? It's our duty to do everything we can do make sure she feels welcome ...

*The others look at Blanche with a murderous glance. Harold offers his arm to Blanche who takes it only to piss off the other two.*

**Harold** – Allow me ...

*Harold leaves the sitting room with Blanche on his arm.*

**Reggie** – First she takes your armchair ... Then she takes your seat at the captain's table ...

**Harriet** – Apparently she used to be an actress.

**Reggie** – And we all know what that means ...

**Harriet** – What does it mean?

**Reggie** – An actress my arse ...

**Harriet** – She won't last long here ...

*The residents are about to leave the sitting room when Harriet, who is puffing up her armchair a little, finds something on the ground.*

**Harriet** – What's this?

**Reggie** – Let me see ... I have no idea ...

**Harriet** – A disposable thermometer?

**Reggie** – It doesn't look like anything I ever stuck in any of my holes.

**Harriet** – No, not a thermometer, there's no graduation for the temperature ...

**Reggie** – Don't tell me it's a sex toy ...

**Harriet** – I think it might be a pregnancy test ...?

**Reggie** – You're right ... There's two lines ...

**Harriet** – Two lines? Does that mean there's a bun in someone's oven?

**Reggie** – Who knows ... It's the first time I see one of those ...

**Harriet** – Back in our day we didn't need these fancy gadgets to know we were up the duff ... We'd need the manual ...

**Reggie** – Or we could ask someone. Who might be pregnant?

**Harriet** – In a care home? We can start by eliminating quite a few of the women ...

**Reggie** – That leaves the nursing assistants and the director ...

**Harriet** – What about the father, who could it be ...?

*Roberto, the doctor, enters the room. An Italian playboy, in his thirties with a flirtatious attitude.*

**Roberto** – Good morning ... So, how is everyone feeling this morning?

**Reggie** – I'm all right, Doctor ...

**Roberto** – And what about yourself, my dear? Look at this complexion! Peaches and cream, like a young girl! What is the secret of your eternal youth?

**Harriet** – They spliced jellyfish genes in our cells.

**Reggie** – I'd keep my distance if I were you, you could get stung and break out in hives ...

**Roberto** – And how is the new hip, Reggie?

**Reggie** – It's all right.

**Roberto** – So we can look at doing the second one, then? You know my clinic is running a promotion on hip replacements at the moment. The second is half price. But you need to make a decision soon.

**Harriet** – At our age, you know ...

**Reggie** – It's like with old cars. You need to take everything into consideration before starting on more repairs.

**Harriet** – You replace the brakes and a week later the engine burns out ...

**Roberto** – Come now, my dear, anyone can tell your engine is still purring under that hood! You've got the body of a Ferrari!

*The residents are slowly starting to get ready to leave.*

**Harriet** – Unfortunately, we're more like those vintage cars that no one wants to take out for a spin ...

**Reggie** – For fear that they break down before reaching the end of the street ...

**Harriet** – We've reached our mileage limit, my good man.

**Reggie** – At least we were able to enjoy a bit of the second-hand market before ending up here, at the junkyard. But you, with the current 68-year-old state pension requirement, you went straight from school to the workplace, and from there you'll go straight to residential care.

**Harriet** – Or hopefully directly from the workplace to the cemetery, and spare society the cost of your state pension ...

**Reggie** – Especially since you spent all these years in medical school and didn't start working and paying pension contributions until much later.

**Harriet** – Look at the bright side ... you already work in a care home, so you'll just have to swap your lab coat and fancy shoes for a ratty jumper and slippers.

**Reggie** – You think we're dependant ... but are we really that different? Do you really think working ten hours a day for your boss's benefit, for half a century, isn't being dependant?

*The residents prepare to exit the room, leaving Roberto a little disconcerted by this exchange.*

**Roberto** – I'm not chasing you away, am I.

**Reggie** – It's almost lunch time.

**Harriet** – We're going to freshen up a little, try to make ourselves presentable. So our appearance doesn't put anyone off their food.

**Reggie** – It's hard enough to maintain an appetite when we see what's being served in our plates ...

**Roberto** – Right ... Well, bon appetit, then!

*The residents leave. The director enters.*

**Natalie** *(preoccupied)* – Oh, Roberto, I was just looking for you ...

*He goes to her and tries to take her into his arms.*

**Roberto** – You look radiant this morning, Natalie!

**Natalie** *(shrugging him away)* – Please, Roberto, not here ... Someone could see us ...

**Roberto** – So what ...? We're getting married, remember.

**Natalie** – We haven't announced it officially yet ...

**Roberto** – We're in love, that's all that matters. And I told you before. With your care home and my private clinic we're going to make a killing, Natalie!

**Natalie** – Of course ... Even if our primary mission remains the wellbeing and happiness of our dear elderly residents.

**Roberto** – Of course, naturally. And what did you want to tell me that was so important, my dear?

**Natalie** – Well ... It's a little awkward actually ... I'm not one hundred percent sure yet ...

**Roberto** – Are you free for dinner?

*They start to leave together.*

**Natalie** – Yes, let's talk about it later ...

*They leave.*

***Black.***

# The afternoon

*In the sitting room, Harriet, who has reclaimed her armchair, is knitting with a sullen look on her face. Reggie, wearing a cap, is sitting next to her.*

**Reggie** – Come now, don't sulk Harriet ... I'm sure another place will free up soon at the Captain's table ...

**Harriet** – I bloody hope so ...

**Reggie** – What are you knitting? A scarf?

**Harriet** – It's a surprise ...

**Reggie** – Who's it for?

**Harriet** – Maybe for you ...

*Blanche enters with Harold.*

**Reggie** – So tell me Blanche, how did you like the restaurant?

**Blanche** – The restaurant? No idea, we had lunch in the canteen ...

**Harold** – We call it the restaurant here ...

**Blanche** – I can tell you haven't been to a restaurant in a long while. *(To Harriet)* What is the sea-cow knitting? A net? Are you planning on going deep-sea fishing?

**Reggie** – It's a scarf, I think.

**Blanche** – Not for me, I hope.

**Harriet** – Who knows ...

**Reggie** – It's a surprise.

**Harold** – It looks more like a rope, doesn't it?

**Reggie** – A rope made of wool?

**Harold** – That way whoever uses it to hang themselves won't catch a cold.

*Caroline enters the room with the latest issue of* Blue Rinse Life.

**Caroline** – Here you go, something to read ... The latest issue of *Blue Rinse Life*, like every Wednesday ...

*To Harriet's dismay, Blanche grabs the magazine before she has a chance to take it.*

**Blanche** – I'll finally find out if I won ...

*Caroline starts doing some light house cleaning.*

**Caroline** – I love what you're knitting ... What is it?

**Harold** – We don't know.

**Caroline** – It looks very snug and warm.

**Harriet** – What matters is that it's strong ...

**Caroline** – Oh, yes, that too, of course.

**Reggie** – When you're done you should start on booties for the baby ...

**Caroline** – The baby? Whose baby?

**Harriet** – That's what we'd like to know ...

*Blanche thumbs through the magazine when suddenly her face lights up.*

**Blanche** – It's mine!

**Reggie** – What's yours?

**Blanche** – The prize! From the competition in *Blue Rinse Life*! My entry was selected in the draw! I won the cruise!

**Reggie** – First prize? The cruise in the Pacific islands? On the Cuesta Mucho?

**Blanche** – No, second prize! The cruise in Antarctica! On the Cuesta Poco!

**Harold** – But that's fantastic news! You're very lucky!

**Harriet** – Lucky at cards ...

**Blanche** – Actually, it's a trip for two, so ... I can take whoever I want ... Put that in your pipe and smoke it ...

**Reggie** – What could you possibly do on a ship in Antarctica? They won't even have a swimming pool ...

**Harriet** – They might have a skating rink.

**Caroline** – Why would you even want to go on a vacation? Aren't you permanently on vacation here?

**Blanche** – For the change of scenery! It smells stale here ...

**Reggie** – It's true it's getting a bit hot. *(He removes his cap, places it on an armchair and wipes his brow.)* And who will be your plus one, Blanche?

**Blanche** – No idea ...

**Harold** – Well, if you need a knight in shining armor ...

**Blanche** – Shining armor? What use would that be to me, you old fart. Would you even be able to carry my suitcase?

*Roberto enters and discretely tries to either hug or grope Caroline, who shrugs him off.*

**Roberto** – You all look very cheerful! What's going on?

**Harriet** – Blanche won a cruise. In Antarctica.

*Roberto doesn't seem to take this project very seriously.*

**Roberto** – Excellent, excellent ...

**Harriet** – Oh, Doctor, can I have a word?

**Roberto** – Of course Harriet, I am all ears.

**Harriet** – Privately ...

**Roberto** (*reluctantly*) – Of course ...

*She takes him aside and shows him the pregnancy test.*

**Harriet** – Does this mean pregnant or not pregnant?

**Roberto** (*gobsmacked*) – You're pregnant, Harriet?

**Harriet** – Not me! We found it in one of the armchairs this morning ...

**Roberto** – Really?

**Harriet** – As you can imagine ... It can't be one of your residents ...

*Roberto appears worried.*

**Roberto** – Can you leave this with me, Harriet? I'd like to investigate a little ...

**Harriet** – Of course, but keep me informed ...?

**Caroline** – It's nap time. Everyone in bed!

**Blanche** – Nap time? But I'm not sleepy.

**Caroline** – Rules are rules ...

**Harold** – Sir, yes Sir ... You're right, Blanche, it's very much like the barracks here.

**Blanche** – Really? They have mandatory afternoon delight in the marine infantry too?

*The residents leave the room. Reggie accidentally leaves his cap on the armchair.*

**Roberto** – Are you the one that's pregnant, Caroline?

**Caroline** – Pardon?

**Roberto** – Is this yours?

*He shows her the pregnancy test.*

**Caroline** – And what if it was?

**Roberto** – Don't tell me you're thinking of keeping it?

**Caroline** – No, I'm planning on donating it to the Salvation Army. For those who are less fortunate than me.

**Roberto** – Listen Caroline, what happened between us was ... a moment of weakness.

**Caroline** – A moment of weakness that's coming back quite strongly, if I judge by the result of this pregnancy test.

*Natalie arrives. Caroline leaves.*

**Roberto** – Oh good, I wanted to talk to you.

**Natalie** – Yes, me too ...

**Roberto** – Are you pregnant?

**Natalie** – My God, no! Why?

**Roberto** – I'm sorry, I don't know why I said that ...

*Reggie comes back for his cap. They don't notice his presence so he decides to stay and eavesdrop.*

**Natalie** – No, what's worrying me is that ... the mortality rate in our establishment has increased in unusually high proportions recently. Haven't you noticed?

**Roberto** – I have ... Mortality rates in care homes are typically higher than birth rates, but not in these proportions ...

**Natalie** – What birth?

**Roberto** – Come to think of it, care homes also tend to experience fewer violent deaths than police stations or schools in North London ...

**Natalie** – You're worrying me, Roberto. If you know something, you have to tell me ...

**Roberto** – It's about Delia.

**Natalie** – Delia?

**Roberto** – It would seem that her death ... may not have been entirely natural.

**Natalie** – What makes you say that?

**Roberto** – I can't be sure of course, but I have uncovered some evidence that make me think that she ...

**Natalie** – What evidence?

**Roberto** – Well, the strangulation marks I noticed around her neck, for starters.

**Natalie** – What...?

**Roberto** – And then ... There's the fork from the canteen that I found stuck in her abdomen.

**Natalie** – Oh, my God...!

**Roberto** – We would need to carry out a full autopsy to find out if she hasn't been poisoned as well.

**Natalie** – Who would want to kill a hundred-and-three-year-old resident?

**Roberto** – A hundred-and-two-year-old resident who wants to have a shot at being the oldest living person in the world ...?

**Natalie** – This is all really quite unpleasant, Roberto. The very reputation of our establishment is at stake. Can you imagine? If this all came to the media's attention!

**Roberto** – After the remarkable work you did to get us such a high ranking in the Michelin Guide of Care Homes ...

**Natalie** – We'd immediately lose our third Gold Denture, the one awarded to care homes with more than twenty centenarians.

**Roberto** – And probably our third fork, too ...

**Natalie** – Do you think we should notify the authorities regardless?

**Roberto** – Maybe ... I'm not sure ... After all, the law doesn't consider it a crime to take the life of a three-month old fetus. If you push this reasoning a little further ... it's not that far-fetched to think that ending the agony of a hundred-and-three year old woman isn't really a crime either ...

**Natalie** – It is for our religious laws, Roberto!

**Roberto** – So what do we do? Do we shoot ourselves in the foot and notify them?

**Natalie** – You're right ... It's probably best if we start by conducting our own little private investigation ...

**Roberto** – I agree with you, Natalie ... You can count on me. After all, we're getting married, aren't we?

**Natalie** – For better and for worse ...

**Roberto** – We just need to find out who did it and why.

**Natalie** – Do you think the murderer could be one of the staff?

**Roberto** – It's a possibility ... But why?

**Natalie** – Euthanasia? It's all the rage these days ...

**Roberto** – I can't see a nurse strangling an old dear with one hand, while stabbing her with a fork in the other. Generally speaking, euthanasia is an act of love performed towards our fellow man, isn't it?

**Natalie** – Listen to you ... You know the Pope is categorically against these practices.

**Roberto** – The Church will change its position on that too, like it did on many other subjects ... Give it five or ten centuries, you'll see ... Euthanasia ... Although the word itself doesn't help ...

**Natalie** – How do you mean?

**Roberto** – You can't spell euthanasia without nazi ... In fact, they're the ones who first industrialised the concept, unfortunately. So good luck reclaiming it now ...

**Natalie** – And what would you call it, to make the practice more readily accepted?

**Roberto** – I don't know, do I ... Something less ... Or more ...

*Blanche walks past carrying a suitcase. Reggie scarpers, for fear of being discovered.*

**Natalie** – Where do you think you're going, Blanche?

**Blanche** – I'm leaving for my cruise, aren't I.

**Natalie** – No, but wait, you can't just leave.

**Blanche** – Why not?

**Natalie** – I have to let your father know. I mean, your son ...

**Roberto** – Someone has to sign discharge papers.

**Blanche** – Discharge? Who are you calling a discharge?

**Natalie** *(to Roberto)* – I'll go notify the family ...

**Roberto** – Come now, Blanche, you can't leave us like that. Can't this wait until tomorrow? Why don't you go and take a nice stroll outside while I take your suitcase back to your room ...

**Blanche** – You're trying to lead me up the garden path, aren't you?

**Roberto** – Those cruise ships are full of seniors, you know ... I'm not sure you'd notice any difference with the retirement home.

*Blanche sits, grudgingly. Roberto leaves with her suitcase. Harold and Harriet enter.*

**Harold** – You look upset, Blanche, what's going on?

**Harriet** – Can we do anything?

**Blanche** – I'm eighty-six years old, can you do anything about that?

**Harold** – Eighty-six! You look exceptional for your age.

**Harriet** – I would have said eighty, at the most.

*Reggie enters.*

**Reggie** – Did you hear?

**Harriet** – Yes, for the last time, I can hear just fine.

**Reggie** – Delia was murdered!

**Harriet** – No?

**Reggie** – I heard it from the director ...

**Harriet** – She told you that?

**Reggie** – Let's just say I was at the right place at the right time. Anyway, there's a serial killer among us!

**Harold** – How do they know it's one of us?

**Reggie** – Who would want to come to an old people's home just to murder the elderly?

**Harold** – That's true ... I could understand if they targeted a children's summer camp, but a retirement home ...

**Harriet** – A serial killer?

**Reggie** – Well, hundred-year-old residents have been dropping like flies around here ... Haven't you noticed?

**Harold** – Who could it be ...?

**Harriet** – A staff member, surely ...

*Caroline enters.*

**Caroline** – Who's up for a lovely cup of herbal tea to help with their digestion? Chamomile? Peppermint? Rosehip?

**Reggie** – Could the killer be ... a woman?

**Harold** – No, thank you, not for me.

**Reggie** – Not for me either, thank you ...

**Caroline** – Looks like there aren't any takers today ... Too bad ...

*Caroline leaves.*

**Reggie** – Chamomile, my arse ... More like hemlock ...

**Blanche** – And they say I'm the crazy one.

**Reggie** – What do you care, you're going on a cruise!

**Harold** – Speaking of which, who are you taking as your plus one?

**Reggie** – Are you pushing this because you're afraid of staying here, Captain?

**Harriet** – But the Captain should always be the last one to leave the ship! I remember this one time on the Titanic ...

**Blanche** – I see the Antarctic cruise is very popular all of a sudden.

**Reggie** – Better than staying here and getting bumped off.

**Blanche** – We could draw a name ...

**Reggie** – Let's all put our names on bits of paper in Harold's hat, and then we'll draw one.

**Harold** – Good idea ...

*Harold removes his hat. They all write something on pieces of paper that they place in the hat, in deadly silence, all while casting suspicious glances at each other.*

**Harriet** – An honest hand for the draw?

**Blanche** – You'll have to make do with mine.

*Everyone is tense. She pulls a piece of paper out of the hat and unfolds it.*

**Blanche** – Reggie.

*Reggie appears relieved.*

**Reggie** – I'd like to express good luck wishes to those who will remain behind ...

*Caroline returns, followed closely by Roberto.*

**Caroline** – What's going on here? What's with the conspiracy faces?

**Reggie** – We were playing a game of Clue ... You know how it is. Things always get out of hand.

**Caroline** – Oh …? And who did it?

**Harriet** – We haven't finished playing yet. We only know the crime took place in the bedroom with a fork.

**Reggie** – Mmm ... I don't remember telling you about that ...

*Harold puts his hat back on and everyone leaves. In a low voice, Roberto picks up where he left off with Caroline.*

**Roberto** – But Caroline, be reasonable, you can't keep it ...

**Caroline** – Why not?

**Roberto** – You know I'm going to marry Natalie.

**Caroline** – You should have thought about that before ... Maybe I should tell her you're about to become a dad?

**Roberto** – How many times?

**Caroline** – I didn't say I was having triplets.

**Roberto** – I mean, how many times will you make me beg ... Alright, how much do you want to get rid of it?

**Caroline** – Twenty k?

**Roberto** – Ten.

**Caroline** – Ok. But I want the dosh now.

*Roberto pulls out his cheque book, writes a cheque and hands it to her.*

**Roberto** – Do I have your word?

**Caroline** – As long as the cheque doesn't bounce ...

*Caroline leaves.*

**Roberto** – Right, that's done, one less thing to worry about ... And it's a bargain compared to child support ...

*He leaves too. Blanche returns, followed by Christian.*

**Christian** – So, Mum, what's this I hear about a cruise?

**Blanche** – Why wouldn't I be allowed to go on a vacation?

**Christian** – Come now, Mum, you're too old to take part in an expedition in Antarctica.

**Blanche** – Cruises are made for old people! Why else do you think they advertise in *Blue Rinse Life*?

**Christian** – Yes, sure, but ... There's old and there's old ... And anyway, cruises are dangerous, sometimes the ships capsize. There's at least one shipwreck a month, somewhere in the world.

**Blanche** – At my age, I live every day with the threat of being shipwrecked, knowing that my chances of survival dwindle with every day that goes by.

**Christian** – You always focus on the negative side of things. Aren't you happy here?

**Blanche** – What? Haven't you heard?

**Christian** – Heard what?

**Blanche** – It's like being in a slasher film! The doctor is performing genetic experiments on the residents and the nursing assistant is a serial killer!

*Natalie enters.*

**Natalie** – Listen, I checked in *Blue Rinse Life* magazine, and the competition results haven't even been published yet.

**Christian** – Are you sure?

**Natalie** – I even called them to get confirmation ...

**Christian** *(to Blanche)* – But Mum, why did you make up this story about a cruise?

**Blanche** – Oh, I don't know ... It's boring as fuck around here ... I thought I'd do something to stir things up a little ...

**Christian** – Well congratulations, it worked.

**Natalie** – I'm sorry to have called you for nothing ...

**Christian** – No, please, I'm the one who's sorry ... Although, I did warn you... She likes to ham it up ...

**Natalie** – I'll take her back to her room.

*Christian kisses his mother goodbye.*

**Christian** – Goodbye, Mum...

**Blanche** *(in a low voice)* – The part about the serial killer, that's true, I swear ... You absolutely have to get me out of here ...

**Christian** – But of course ...

**Blanche** *(still in a low voice)* – Call the police ... But don't say anything to the director, she's part of a satanic cult ...

**Christian** – Right, let's do that ...

**Natalie** – Come now Blanche, we're going to take care of you ...

*Natalie takes Blanche by the arm and leads her away. Christian's mobile phone rings and he takes the call.*

**Christian** – Hello? Yes, yes, it's all fine, I'll tell you later ... They're going to give her an injection and she'll sleep soundly until tomorrow morning ... Er, no, I don't know if they actually give them injections, I imagine they do ... That's what I would do, anyway ... *(His expression changes)* You have great news? No, I have no idea and I'm not really in the mood to play charades ... I'm going to be a dad? No ...? Yes, yes, of course I'm deliriously happy ... So you're pregnant, finally ... No, I'm not surprised, but ... Well, at your age ... The doctor told you it would require a miracle. And you're really sure? You didn't read the pregnancy test wrong? I'd like to see it when I get back, just in case ... You lost it? Where? You don't just lose a pregnancy test ... Here, at the care home when you dropped off my mother's file yesterday? Yes, yes, of course, if I find it I'll bring it back. We can keep it as a souvenir ... Yes, of course I'm happy. But we just managed to find a care home for my mother ... and now we're going to have to start all over again to find a day care center ... Yes, they have waiting lists too! ... Listen, we'll talk more when I get back ... Love you too…

*Christian leaves.*

*Roberto and Natalie enter.*

**Natalie** – And do you suspect anyone in particular?

**Roberto** – One of the nursing assistants maybe ...

**Natalie** – Caroline…?

**Roberto** – Why not?

**Natalie** – You told me you didn't believe in the euthanasia theory, because of the M.O. And you're right, an injection of sodium is so much less messy ...

**Roberto** – Maybe she used a fork to throw us off ...

**Natalie** – Still ... A fork from the canteen ... To end someone's suffering out of compassion ...

**Roberto** – She could have been hired by someone. For money.

**Natalie** – You think she could be a hitman?

**Roberto** – I have it on good authority that Caroline is perfectly capable of killing for money.

**Natalie** – But who would want the death of a hundred-year-old woman? The heirs to her estate? They knew she only had a few months left ... at the most ... They couldn't be in that much of a hurry ...

**Roberto** – How about those whose parents are on our waiting list...? Most people would be willing to kill for a place in a day care center. So imagine for a care home ...

**Natalie** – Blanche's son ...?

**Roberto** – Or his partner.

**Natalie** – There is something strange about her, I agree.

**Roberto** – Hmm ... I'd say she's downright odd, even.

**Natalie** – Ok, but we can't lose sight of the other possibilities ... Do you have any new elements regarding the victim?

**Roberto** – The summary autopsy I performed with whatever I found in the kitchen show that Delia died after eating a plate of spagbol.

**Natalie** – Do you think she could have died from food poisoning as well?

**Roberto** – I don't think so ... I had the same spagbol last night and I'm still alive.

**Natalie** – Anything else worth mentioning?

**Roberto** – Yes ... Before she was stabbed with one of the canteen forks in the stomach, Delia was strangled with a hand-knitted scarf ... I found some wool fibres in the creases of her neck ...

**Natalie** – Hand-knitted ... That is an interesting fact indeed… I think we should also be interrogating the residents.

**Roberto** – Let's do it after dinner, then ... They're all in the restaurant right now ...

**Natalie** – What's on the menu tonight?

**Roberto** – Spaghetti bolognese.

**Natalie** – Again!

**Roberto** – There were leftovers from yesterday. And since most of them can't remember what they had for dinner from one day to the next ...

**Natalie** – Let's order Chinese takeout then.

***Black.***

# Evening

*The set is the same as before but it now looks like something between a police interrogation room and a Gestapo office. Roberto and Natalie are sitting in armchairs. Roberto is holding chopsticks and eating Chinese food from a cardboard takeout container, American series-style. Natalie is the bad cop and proceeds to roughly interrogate Reggie, who is wearing striped pyjamas and is sitting in a wheelchair (if possible) with a desk lamp shining in his face. Natalie has turned into a natural-born torturer. She is waiving the fork, which is their main piece of evidence.*

**Natalie** – So you admit having seen this fork from the canteen before.

**Reggie** – Well, yeah.

**Natalie** – On the crime scene?

**Reggie** – Well, no.

**Natalie** – Oh really? Where, then?

**Reggie** – Well, in the canteen!

**Natalie** – Don't fuck with me, Reggie.

**Reggie** – It's a fork from the canteen! Look, there's still some bolognaise sauce on it.

**Roberto** *(intervening)* – That, my dear Reggie, is not bolognaise sauce, believe me.

**Reggie** *(yawning)* – I wouldn't mind going to bed now, I'm getting really sleepy ...

**Natalie** – I'm not in a rush. I can go all night long if we need to.

**Reggie** – It's just that I'm used to lights out at eight thirty.

**Natalie** – Ok, let's start from the top. State your full name, profession, date and place of birth ...

**Reggie** – Can I have my herbal now? I always have my herbal when I'm watching my cop show.

**Natalie** *(losing it)* – Spill the beans, motherfucker!

*Roberto tries to control her with a hand gesture and, playing the good cop, takes over the interrogation.*

**Roberto** – Come on, Reggie. You know me… I'm on your side. I'm your doctor. Why don't you just tell me everything you know ...

**Reggie** – About what?

**Roberto** – Well, for example, have you seen anyone knit something recently?

**Reggie** – I saw Harriet knitting a scarf ... that looked a lot like a rope.

*Roberto and Natalie exchange glances.*

**Roberto** – Harriet ...

**Natalie** – But why would she have done it?

**Roberto** *(to Reggie)* – Did Harriet have any reason to want Delia dead?

**Reggie** – Well ... She's been eyeing the captain's table for a long time, hasn't she.

**Roberto** – But of course ...! Delia dead, Harriet gets a seat at the table, that tracks ...

**Natalie** – Harriet ... But she looks like butter wouldn't melt ...

**Roberto** – So now we need to get her to spill the beans ... Whether or not she sits at the captain's table ...

**Natalie** – You can go to your room now, Reggie ... You've done your duty ...

*Reggie checks his watch.*

**Reggie** – It doesn't matter, my cop show is over now ... I've been watching every episode for weeks and you made me miss the final where they reveal who did it...

**Roberto** – Let's go get Harriet ... Before she kills someone else.

*Natalie and Roberto leave. Reggie, despondent, sits in an armchair and starts reading* Blue Rinse Life. *Harriet enters, her knitted scarf in her hands.*

**Harriet** – Say, Reggie, aren't you a lucky bugger! You're Blanche's plus one. For the cruise ...

**Reggie** – Just between you and I, I am relieved, it's true. I'm terrified they'll poison us ... I don't think the spagbol are agreeing with me.

**Harriet** – I know what you mean ... Delia found it difficult to stomach it too ...

**Reggie** – Which is strange because I love that dish ... Shame they don't serve it more often ... So that's it, your scarf is done?

**Harriet** – Yes.

**Reggie** – Who is it for?

**Harriet** – For you! You're going to need a scarf for that cruise in Antarctica. Let me help you with it.

*Harriet stands up and strangles Reggie from behind, but she is interrupted by Natalie and Roberto who return and, witnessing the scene, see their suspicions confirmed.*

**Roberto** – Caught red handed …!

**Natalie** – Reggie, could you give us a minute, please.

**Reggie** – But ...

**Roberto** – Fuck off to your room!

*Reggie leaves.*

**Roberto** – And now Reggie ... But why?

**Harriet** – To take his place on the cruise! I've always loved cruises. Did I mention I was on the Titanic when it sunk?

**Roberto** – What are we going to do with her?

**Natalie** – I don't know.

**Roberto** – Do you see us turning her in to the cops, at her age?

**Natalie** – On the other hand, knitting the murder weapon is indicative of a certain level of premeditation.

**Harriet** – I heard that pleading senile dementia had very successful outcomes ...

**Roberto** – Maybe we should handle this internally ...

**Natalie** – How old are you, Harriet?

**Harriet** – I just celebrated my hundredth birthday last week ...

**Natalie** – If they take her away, we only have nineteen centenarian pensioners left ... and we lose our third Golden Dentures from the Michelin Guide to Care Homes…

**Roberto** – You're one lucky bitch, you know that ...

**Natalie** – Until another pensioner receives their hundredth birthday card from the King ...

**Harriet** – Not if something happens to them first ...

*Natalie and Roberto look at her, worried.*

***Black.***

# A year later

*Natalie, Roberto and Caroline are seated in three of the armchairs, looking extremely tired, or even prematurely aged.*

**Natalie** – I've got nothing left ...

**Roberto** – And it's barely noon ...

**Caroline** – They'll be the death of us ...

**Natalie** – Can't wait for retirement ...

*The four residents enter the room, looking considerably younger than before.*

**Reggie** – Look at you!  You all look like death!

**Roberto** – You, on the other hand, look positively sprightly after this cruise.

**Blanche** – That's right, we're in top shape, aren't we Captain?

**Harold** – We feel twenty years younger.

**Reggie** – This is going to end with a wedding, mark my words ...

**Harriet** – And those anti-ageing products with jellyfish extract you brought back ...

**Reggie** – Right...? Nothing short of spectacular!

*Christian arrives with a Moses basket which we assume holds a baby.*

**Christian** – Hello everyone ...

**Natalie** – Sir ...

**Christian** – Madam the Director ... How are you? You look a little tired ...

**Natalie** – You were right. They'll bury us all ...

**Christian** – Mum, meet your grandson.

**Blanche** – Oh, right ... Why is he all scrunched up like that...?

**Harriet** – It's true, he's got even more wrinkles than we do.

**Harold** – I hope he's in better shape than he looks.

**Reggie** – Because he's going to be working to pay for our retirement…

**Harold** – Say, you look tired too ...?

**Christian** – He's not sleeping through the night yet, the little turkey ...

**Harriet** – Lower your voices everyone, can't you see he's asleep.

**Harold** – He looks like his dad, don't you think?

**Blanche** – So, er, what can we wish for this child?

**Harriet** – Captain, a word of welcome for the babe?

*Harold clears his throat and starts a speech.*

**Harold** – "Age doesn't matter, unless you are a cheese" said Kim Kardashian quoting Luis Buñuel. Life is like a cruise on the *Titanic*: whether you're nibbling canapes on the top deck or slurping soup in the hold, at the end of the day we're all destined to feed the fishes. So, as we wait for the inevitable iceberg, those of us who still can, might as well sit back, enjoy the orchestra and the sound of ice clinking in our glasses.

*They toast.*

**Everyone** *(in the direction of the Moses basket)* – Welcome aboard!

*Music. They start dancing a waltz.*

**Black.**

### *The End*

*February 2023*